RISE OF THE DOLOCHER

European P. Douglas

GHOST CREATIVE

Contents

PART 1

The Fall

CHAPTER 1

The fall of Erskine Chambers began with the debt of £15,000 lost at cards. It hadn't been his first enormous loss, but was by far the biggest and the one that broke his elderly father's faith in him. Disinherited and cast out, he had to start to make his own way in the world, penniless and with no skills to speak of.

As he left the family estate with only the clothes on his back and the horse he rode, he never looked back. London was the obvious place to go first. His friends advised just this,

'Give your father time to cool down, he'll forgive you and take you back in before you know it.'

What they didn't know was that Erskine didn't want forgiveness. His life had been mundane in the extreme at home, and the drinking and gambling had been his only escape. Now that he had been cast out, he'd never felt so free. He meant to leave and never come back. Instead of heading for London, Erskine made his way to the West. There was no plan in mind, and no destination to aim for. He would travel and see what the world would throw at him.

It wasn't long before the world threw something at him.

A few days later, as he walked a lonely road in the countryside, two men emerged from behind a tree. The first grabbed the bridle of the horse and the second stood out in a fighting stance, a knife held in his hand.

"Give us what you have and there's no need for you to get hurt," the one with the knife said. Though fear was the first thing to grip Erskine, he couldn't help but laugh at the absurdity of this.

"You can't steal from a penniless man," he said.

The two men didn't seem to see the humour in it,

"A penniless man doesn't have a horse like this," the one holding the bridle said.

"Nor clothes like what you're wearing?" the other said. Erskine looked over both his clothes and his horse and though he thought nothing special of them, when he looked at the tatty rags on his oppressors, he could see the marked difference. It was then that the anger came now that he saw the genuine threat of violence.

Erskine had been in a few punch ups before, but only ever with men of his own class and never ever with weapons. These men didn't look the type to be worried about breaking the rules or dishonouring themselves.

"Get down off the horse," the man with the knife said. Erskine looked around, thinking about his options. If he kicked hard on the horse, it might bolt, but then the man at the front might get a good hold of Erskine and pull him down. He thought it best to give up what he had without a fight. It wouldn't make him much worse off than he already was. He eased off down to the ground.

The man holding the horse moved it off the road and tied it to a tree while Erskine stood there, guarded by the other man.

"I think it's time we had a look in those pockets, don't you Trev?" the large man by the horse said. He was coming over to Erskine now with a strange, scowled smile on his face, an expression that Erskine had never seen in any face before now.

"Empty 'em," the other man said. Erskine looked to him following the spoken voice and at that moment he felt the hardest blow he'd ever receive smash into the underside of his jaw.

Everything went white for a moment and then black blurry blobs came over his vision as he realised he was on the ground. A heavy boot came into his stomach then, hard enough that he doubled over like a baby in the womb. He could hear the horses whinnying and stamping about, and then a foot made contact with the back of his head. This dazed him more, and he felt like he was losing consciousness.

"Penniless man, my arse!" the one called Trev called out, mocking him.

"Those shoes look like they cost a bob or two," the other man said. Erskine felt his shoes being pulled from his feet, but he was powerless to do anything about it. He felt invasive hands run through his clothes, looking for things that were not there.

"He's got nothing on him, Gary!" Trev cried in what sounded like childish disbelief. Rougher hands ran over him and then Gary's voice came loud and clear.

"Damn it!" and another sharp kick to the face was delivered. This time Erskine was sure he lost consciousness.

When he woke sometime later, Erskine Chambers was not the same man as before. His face was tight and swollen and when his hands went to his cheeks, they stung like fire; sticky blood covered the tips of his fingers. Wincing in pain, he put one hand back to feel again and knew that while he'd been out cold, they had sliced cuts in his cheeks, cuts that were deep and wide and felt like they would last him a lifetime.

Tears flowed from his eyes and stung his wounds further. They were not, however, tears of pain but of sorrow. He'd never been a particularly vain man, but he already knew that this scarred face would be his life from now on. People would treat him differently at first glance, children would run from him and woman would move away when he came close. He'd seen vagrants with gnarled faces before and how even he himself had treated them in the past. He could only hope that what he felt didn't look as bad as he feared. Though he didn't see how that could be.

CHAPTER 2

Some weeks later, still looking the worse for wear, Chambers came into the harbour town of Bristol. His clothes had been reduced to rags, and the shoes he wore now were stolen and a little too big for him. It made for uncomfortable waking and his back had started to twist as a result. He looked for all the world like he was on his way to becoming one of those people everyone both despised and felt sorry for, in equal measure; an outcast from society.

What made him different, though, was that he had drive and determination. He had every intention of making a lot of money, more even than he had ever lost, and he intended to do it entirely on his own terms. No one was ever going to tell him what to do or scold him for his actions ever again. He wasn't fully sure how he was going to do it just yet, but he knew he only needed a little to get started and he would be on his way. There was always money to be made in a large town, and he was sure Bristol would be no different.

As luck would have it, his first coin came when a man in a passing carriage took pity on him as he rested at the side of the road. It was a clean shilling, and Chambers was very glad to have it. No sooner did he have it in his hand than he went to a pub, had some food and some ale as he thought about how to turn the rest into more money. Cards were the obvious choice, but he didn't know if the lower classes even played cards, and if they did, how much could they possibly have to bet with? Still, he was in the same boat as they right now and if they played, he would bet whatever they bet to get started.

There turned out to be a great deal of gambling going on in Bristol for those who didn't seem able to afford it. Everything was bet on — dog racing, cockfights, fist fights, feats of strength. It didn't matter; no matter what was going on, someone was willing to place a bet on it. Within three days, Chambers had four pounds. A day later he was back down to one, but a week later his clothes were in better condition. He had shoes that fit, and fifteen pounds weighted his pockets. This was enough to get in into the back room of the 'Grim Reaper' pub.

The 'Grim Reaper' was a place where no one could be trusted. Any ill meaning or ill-tempered person entering the town would find themselves soon drawn to the pub. Fights and violence were a common occurrence, and the barkeeper was more than capable of throwing the fists himself after a skinful of his own booze. In the backroom, those with the money to pay but with manners that excluded them from other backrooms gathered every evening. Tonight, Erskine Chambers was amongst them.

Three other men completed the table this far. To Chambers' right was a man he'd seen betting on dogfights called Martin. He always looked cool and composed, whether he was winning or losing. The man directly across was also familiar to Chambers, but he couldn't put a name to this man. They exchanged a nod of greeting as they sat down. The last man was a large Irish fella, a big grin on his face, and his eyes sparkled with mischief. Chambers had never seen this man before.

One more man came in just before the game was about to start. He was shown to the table by the barman's son, who left just as quickly.

"Good evening, gentlemen," this man said, and he looked around the table, "You are a new face to me?" he said to Chambers, holding out a hand, "Thomas Olivier," he introduced himself. Chambers looked up and took the man's hands. He was clearly a man of Chambers' own former class.

"Chambers," he told the man, ashamed suddenly to mention his full name in case this Thomas fellow had heard of it.

"Good to meet you," the man said and then he saw Chambers' face and he tutted. "I see you came in from the east and met the Cary Brothers." Chambers assumed this was the men who had robbed and beaten him, though he had heard nothing about them up to now.

"I don't know who they were," was all he answered.

"They did that to your face?"

"Yes."

"Then it was them alright," Thomas said. "They aren't actually all that scary in the grand scheme of things, but they are an unpleasant pair," he added, and then took up the deck of cards and checked them over. They seemed to his satisfaction, and he smiled and put them back down.

"Let's play then?" the Irishman asked and play they did.

The night wore on and money ebbed and flowed in front of each man until there were only Olivier and Chambers left. The bet was up to fifty pounds, and Chambers wasn't sure of his hand at all. Olivier smiled at Chambers' nervousness; it was obvious the richer man didn't consider losing fifty pounds to be of any consequence at all.

Chambers took up another card and though it did nothing for his hand, he let a momentary rise of a smile in the corner of his mouth before correcting it. Olivier looked at him and decided not to take another card.

"Show me," he said pleasantly, laying out his own cards on the table. Chambers' head dropped, and he threw his cards down in disappointment. He had lost everything he'd gained tonight and everything he'd brought with him as well. The other men left knowing that this was the end of the entertainment, but when they left the room, Olivier said,

"I like a man who is willing to take a chance, Chambers," and he pushed the entire pot of money over the table to him. "I don't need this," he laughed and stood up.

"But you won?" Chambers said.

"I always win," Olivier replied, pulling on his overcoat, "But that's not what I play for. You need to keep playing, you could be very good. I hope you'll make it a sport for me again one day. I want you to use this money to keep on practising." Without another word, he headed for the door.

"Thank you," Chambers managed to say, though he was still stunned and looking at the pile of money on the table.

Chapter 3

The terrible full headed tension of a hangover greeted Chambers at his next waking and so intense was it that for a time he didn't bother looking at his surroundings or notice that the swell and rising of the surrounding room was real and not some part of the aftereffects of alcohol.

"You made it through the night, so," a voice said from nearby, and Chambers turned his head weakly. A man was standing, no, swaying, in a doorway a few feet away.

"I did," he answered while he tried to place this man's face. He couldn't do it. "Where am I?" he asked, sitting up, fresh pain throbbing through his temples.

"You're on the East Spirit," the man said, grinning. "You don't remember?"

"Remember what?"

"You signed up last night, looking for adventure, you said."

"Signed up for what?"

"A life on the high seas!" the man laughed, clearly enjoying himself now. Chambers pulled himself to his feet and lost his balance with the movement of the ship. He could see past the man now and saw only miles of sea in the ship's wake. The man tossed a sheet of paper to him and he picked it up and looked at it. "We got little sense out of you when you came on board, but the best we could make out from your signature was 'Thomas Olocher', is that right?"

Chambers looked down at the paper and saw the mark he'd made, and a brief glimpse of the previous night came to him. Had he been trying to sign as Thomas Olivier? He realized then that this was his chance of complete freedom, an utter break with the past.

"Thomas Olocher, that's right," he said, saying his new name for the first time. He liked how he sounded and how it felt in his mouth. Thomas Olocher was a name that was going to be well known in years to come; he could feel it.

"An odd name," the man said, "I've never heard it before."

"I suppose all names sounds odd the first time you hear them," Olocher said. To this, the man nodded.

"Tarvey," he said, leaning in to offer his hand. They shook.

At that moment, Olocher suddenly recalled all the money he'd had on him at last recollection. He patted his clothes and even felt in his shoes, but there was nothing. He looked at Tarvey in alarm.

"Take it easy," Tarvey said. "You gave us an envelope of money last night to look after for you. It's not gone anywhere, it's safe."

"Where is it?"

"The captain has it."

"How much is it?"

"I think you told us it was fifty pounds, but I can't be sure."

Olocher thought about this; he had a higher number in his head, but he supposed if he got fifty of it back by now, he'd be lucky. It was enough to be getting on with.

For the rest of the day, Tarvey showed Olocher the ship and introduced him to the men as they went. It was a large ship and was travelling to France for a stop before heading to the Caribbean. His pay would be meagre, but he would have nothing to spend it on and thus it would be a nice lump sum upon landing back in England in six- or seven-months' time. No sooner had he heard this than he knew there would be card games on this boat and his chance to make a lot more than his wages.

He would be taught the positions on the ship and would be expected to do any work assigned to him without question or complaint. Food and drink were provided and there would be plenty of time for 'personal reflection' as well. The look on Tarvey's face as he said this told Olocher it was a euphemism, but for what he could not know. He thought it better not to ask; these things always had a way of revealing themselves soon enough.

The time spent on the 'East Wind' toughened Olocher up and hardened his body. The work was harsh and the conditions brutal, but when he arrived back in Bristol many months later, his body was muscular and strong, his appetite for women and drink had intensified and his pocketbook boasted of £200.

Much of what had made Olocher a 'Gentleman' in his former life, Chambers stripped of him in a matter of months. His hands were no longer soft, and his tongue spoke harsh language as a matter of course. His new physique and the strength he'd gained gave him more confidence in bar rooms and card games, and he felt like he was on his way to achieving his goals. The idea came to him that it didn't matter what anyone else said or did, so long as he himself was happy. And as for how his own happiness affected anyone else? That was becoming of less concern to him day by day.

CHAPTER 4

Maritime skills, gambling skills and confidence were not all Olocher gained while at sea. His general and growing disregard for other people led him to cheating at cards and stealing if the opportunity presented itself. He didn't see this as wrong; it was just all part of his self-advancement. Just something he had to do to keep on the path to riches.

The only problem was that the card players in Bristol had seen all of his tricks before and very soon no decent stake backroom would have him. He railed against each accusation as though it were struck right into his very heart. He was lucky to come away with his life on a couple of occasions. All of this only added to Olocher's sense of frustration and each new person who found him cheating was marked as someone who wanted to keep him down, away from his proper position in society.

One such man was Terrence Glamper, a former soldier and deserter, if he was to be believed. He was the kind of man who always had something to sell or pawn, but at the same time looked like he lived in the alleys and hadn't known a bed or bath since childhood — if even then. He was quick to temper and sometimes picked a man out in a crowd at random and insisted they had slandered him. His fists always flew before the poor victim had even begun to understand the gravity of the situation.

Olocher had seen this man Terrence in action and had heard more than his share of stories about things he hadn't been witness to himself. If that was not enough to make him turn away from the card table once he saw Glamper there, what happened next could almost be called inevitable.

The game was not long in running when the other men at the table claimed they'd lost all they could afford that night and excused themselves. Finally, it was down to Olocher and Glamper. The two men eyed one another over their cards. They were of approximately the same size and to an onlooker it would have looked like Olocher was the more muscled man. Both wore scars and Glamper missed part of an ear, said to have been bitten off in a fight.

No one saw Olocher cheat, or even knew exactly what he'd done, but Glamper seemed to have a sense of it and once it was in his mind, he wouldn't let it go. He reared up furiously, shouting and tossed the card table out of his way, the money and cards spraying everywhere. No one was stupid enough to bend over and try to pocket any of it, though, for fear that Glamper would be after them next.

At first Olocher wasn't too worried; this was, after all, a regular enough scenario for him these days, but then the first blow landed square on his nose — breaking it horribly — and he knew he was in trouble. Springing back from his attacker, Olocher did his best to get to his feet and defend himself, but his legs got tangled in those of the chair and he lost his footing.

"Steal from me, will ya!" Glamper was shouting as he bore down on the falling Olocher. A fist clipped Olocher's cheek in falling, but the stamping foot of Glamper followed it so fast, the sole of his boot met the same broken nose and the back of Olocher's head cracked loudly on the stone floor. A couple of nearby men winced in sympathetic pain and one man ran from the room, not willing to see any more. For a moment, Olocher thought that might be it — generally a man cooled off pretty quickly after a few kicks or punches, but what happened next Olocher would know very little about. The boot came down again and again and after that, he was unconscious.

When he woke up, lucky as he was to wake it all as he was told, his life was never the same again. For a long time, nuns from the local convent cared for him. He could do little for himself and one side of his body was completely paralysed. His vision was blurry and his nose not more than a pouch of gristle now. The worst of it was the shape, the dark shape.

At first, he thought it just an effect of the injuries he'd received, but as his body healed and feeling came back to most of his limbs, he knew that something was not right. When he was alone, it wouldn't be so bad, and his ideas of violence and revenge would be solely aimed at Glamper and the Cary Brothers, but soon, he began to feel what could only be described as hate for the very women who were taking care of him and nursing him back to health.

Each time one of them came to him, Olocher would have to force his mind away from what the dark shape was telling him to do. It didn't have a voice, but that didn't stop it from being persuasive. Images of what could be came to Olocher and, though repulsed by what he saw, he couldn't deny that there was a tingle of excitement and desire there too. Soon Olocher could tell that his thoughts were becoming visible to the women who tended to him. He could see their uneasy looks and how their hands might shake under his gaze. Before long, there were two women in attendance each time. One doing the washing or feeding and the other looking busy. They did not fool Olocher. He would have to leave here soon, though, before he did something he couldn't go back on.

One evening, his last in the convent, one nun attending him was called away by some commotion down the hall. The one remaining looked after her and then glanced up and Olocher. He smiled, but he could feel the evil behind it, and he knew she could see it. She washed him with her head down and he knew she was watching him out of the corner of her eye. His hand clenched into a fist and great anger clouded over him. Though he knew she should be afraid of him, he somehow felt indignant that she was. The dark shape began to change for the first time and a red hue came over his peripheral vision and he could feel his hand lifting slowly. He wanted to bring it down as hard as he could on the back of her head. It felt incredible to have so much power, but to his credit, Thomas Olocher did his best to fight it.

Suddenly, the girl got up and dashed out of the room without looking back or saying a word. She knew what he was thinking; she knew what would happen if she stayed, Olocher thought. He lay back sweating in the bed and took in some deep breaths. He'd come very close to committing the worst act of his life, and he wasn't quite sure how he'd managed to avoid it.

When next someone came to look in on him, Thomas Olocher was gone.

Chapter 5

At first, Thomas Olocher headed east, and he supposed his destination was to be London. If he was ever going to make any real money, that would be the place to do it. He was sure there would be hundreds if not thousands of low-level places to gamble and many more once he began to grow rich and seem more respectable. There were brief thoughts of revenge as he left the convent in Bristol and, though he was sure Glamper would have any number of enemies, Olocher felt he would be caught and arrested if he were to kill him now. It wouldn't leave his mind, however, and the darkness urged him on, telling him to go back and avenge himself, but he fought it. Glamper could wait until the time was right.

Each step closer to London felt wrong, and it wasn't long before Olocher had stopped in the middle of the road. It felt like going home, and he'd promised himself he would never go back home until he'd made a success of himself. His worthless state at present didn't come anywhere near close to qualifying as this. He turned south.

For the next year, Thomas Olocher won money and lost money in almost equal measure. On the whole he was up, but it was so little he would be long in his grave before he made it rich. He still cheated, but only when he was the physically larger of those playing, and he eyed the surrounding men in all games for the threat of violence. The irony in this was that he was the one most likely to spring to violence; the dark shadow always there niggling and telling him that the people around him were either out to get him or could not be trusted.

The scars on his body were added to as he moved from town to town, never staying in one place long enough to make real money because of his temper. It had gotten to the point that he almost blacked out when he was fighting and when he came back to himself, he would see eyes wide with shock and tear-stained faces looking at him as he stood over his mangled opponent. He never knew if any of these people had ever died, but it was true also that he didn't care.

While on the south coast, Olocher got word that the constabulary wanted him for the maiming of a man not too long ago. He decided now was a good time to go back to his work at sea. Going to the docks, he signed up for the first boat that was leaving. He looked on the receding shore of England with relief the very next morning, not knowing for sure if he would ever set foot in his homeland again.

This first attempt at employment, hastily decided upon as it had been, ended badly only days later when he fought a man and viciously broke the man's arm over a drunken slur. The boat docked near Waterford in Ireland and they put Olocher off without pay for his short time. He didn't mind too much; he'd already seen even the hours on that boat that his dark friend would never allow him to live peacefully in that environment. Olocher needed the bustle of a busy city, drinking rooms and ale houses to drown out the dark in him. He knew he was in Ireland now, and the only place in this country he'd ever heard of was Dublin. He recalled someone telling him once about the number of taverns in the city and he felt at once that this was the place for him to head to.

Olocher asked a local how far it was and was dismayed by the distance. He would have to steal a horse as to walk there would take far too long. He could only hope there were some large towns on his way where he could dip into a social noisy scene for time between his lone travels with the darkness.

Thomas Olocher walked for a time before coming across a large manor house with a stable. He waited until dark and went inside and saw that this landowner had no shortage of splendid horses. Skulking about, he took one from a paddocked area that didn't have an enclosure of its own — he imagined the ones with their own 'rooms' as it were, would be the family favourites and thus much more likely to be missed quickly. He took a brown horse from a group comprising mostly brown ones and hoped this would give him the extra time before discovery he would need before he got away. As he took the horse out, he saw what must have been the family crest on the wall of the stable; it was a fearful looking wild boar, and he shuddered at the sight of it.

Having made it off the land and away unhindered, Olocher spent the rest of that night riding in fear of being hunted down. He thought the family he'd stolen from had been too powerful and rich, and it had been a stupid thing to do. They would catch him and make an example of him. It occurred to Olocher that he didn't even know if the laws were the same here in Ireland as they were back home. They might burn people at the stake here for stealing horses for all he knew.

The dark shape didn't help him put his mind at ease, either. It kept feeding him images of a pack of wild boars and dogs bearing down on him. Gaining on him with each mile passed. When they caught up, their masters would do nothing to rein them in and they would watch on as the creatures tore him to shreds.

As soon as he could after light, Olocher swapped this horse for another in a field, moving only the saddle and bridle over and setting the brown one loose. At least now, he didn't feel so pursued. This fresh horse was of much poorer quality and nutrition and whoever owned it would pose no threat to Olocher and the darkness.

Part 2

THE RISE

CHAPTER 6

To his delight, Olocher found Dublin to be just the kind of place he'd been looking for. Dismounting the horse at the old city wall, he left it where it was. He was very surprised that the animal had survived the journey and he didn't expect he'd need it anymore. He thought briefly about taking the saddle and trying to sell it, but as it bore the same wild boar insignia as the stable had, he thought better of it. There was no need to start his time in Dublin on the run from the law.

As he walked, he took in the sounds and smells of the city, seeing riches and poverty in every direction. As he'd been told, there were multiple drinking houses on every street, though he suspected a lot of them were coffee houses and not places where he was going to be able to find card games.

He stepped into a whiskey cabin and was happy to see it almost full in this early afternoon. He ordered a jug and stood at the bar.

"I'm looking for a cheap room," Olocher said to the barman. "Any recommendations?" The barman looked at him a moment and then answered with a smile,

"Take yourself down to Hell and you'll find something." To Olocher, the words sounded like an insult that he was telling him to go to hell, but something in the man's face told different.

"Hell?" Olocher asked cautiously. The barman laughed,

"Sorry, fella," he said, "I heard the accent, and I couldn't resist it." A couple of the men in the room were also laughing, but Olocher didn't turn to look at them; he knew what the dark in him would make of it. "There's a place up the road to the right when you go out, by the Cathedral. It's known locally as Hell," the barman went on. "If you ask around up there, you'll find someone looking to rent a room."

"Thanks," was all Olocher replied as he marvelled at the name of Hell being adjacent to a cathedral. What kind of place had he come to?

After his jug, Thomas Olocher walked up the street as he'd been told, to look for accommodation. He hadn't gotten far when a huge hand planted in the centre of his chest and stopped him dead. Olocher looked up and saw the man's gigantic frame and muscles, his face freshly pulped from a fight.

"With a face like that, you must be used to a fight," the man said.

"What?" Olocher said.

"If you're looking to fight, come and see me. I'm Lord Muc. Ask anyone around and they'll point you in my direction." Without another word, the man removed his hand and walked on. Olocher looked after him and saw him go into the whiskey cabin he'd recently left.

At the top of the road, Olocher entered an archway and came face to face with a statue of the Devil. Again, he couldn't believe it; here he was standing practically in the cathedral's shadow and this was here! Unlit lanterns adorned either side of the statue and he thought how fearful a place this must be at night. He passed through and entered what was known as 'Hell.'

No sooner was he there and looking around than a woman came over to him.

"Are you looking for lodgings, Sir?" Olocher looked at her and found a pleasant face peering into his own. For the first time in a long while, he felt his scars on his face, but she didn't seem to either notice them or be bothered by them.

"Yes, but I have little money as of yet, so it will have to be cheap," he replied. She nodded,

"This is always the case," she smiled. "I'm Paulina. If you want the room, I can show you now?" They talked on price for a moment, and he agreed. It would be well to have a place to stay arranged before he did anything else.

They walked the short distance, and she took him up some stairs and showed him into the room. It turned out to a room in a small apartment that she lived in herself.

"I make a pot every day," Paulina said, pointing at the pot over the fire, "and you can feed yourself from it as you please. I can fix your clothes and wash them if you want, but there is a small charge for this."

"This will do nicely," he said, though he wondered how long she would allow him to stay once he started coming in at all hours and waking her up. "I'll pay for a week up front if that suits you?" he said. He was thinking he could find something else in that time. She nodded and took the coins he offered. As she put the money into her apron, the dark shape spoke into Olocher's ear. 'If you kill her now, you can have the room and take the money back.' It was sly and persuasive, but he knew it was not right. It had a lust for killing that had yet gone unsated, and he would do his best to starve it.

"I'll be coming home quite late most nights," he said.

"That's fine," she said. "You won't be the first lodger I've had who did that."

"I have a niece who will come to stay with me soon," Paulina said, "but she won't be any trouble to you, and I'll keep her to my room at night." Olocher nodded at this, a triviality that made no difference to him at all.

Chapter 7

Olocher soon learned of the violent undertone of the city. An oppressed people had to vent at something, and casual violence was the form this most often took. He found out more about Lord Muc who ran a street gang who fought pitched battles against 'enemies' from across the river. Every Night fights would break out in pubs, taverns, alehouses, and whiskey cabins. It seemed ever the genteel coffeehouses were not immune to fisticuffs during the day.

This, of course, suited Olocher and his darkness down to the ground. He could fight and think nothing of it, feeding the dark shape but not doing anything that went beyond what everyone around him was also doing. He thought about joining Muc's gang, but that would mean making arbitrary enemies that might exclude him from card games on the north side of the Liffey. That was a large pot of money he couldn't block himself from.

One evening — after a two-week lucky streak — in fine clothes, he called to one of the classier brothels. This one was run by a Frenchwoman called Madame Mel and from what he'd heard, she was quite a sight to behold. He was not disappointed when he saw her, but was very deflated when one of the other customers pointed out that she was off limits.

He drank in the main parlour with the other men and the girls from the brothel and eyed up which one he would like to take to her room. As he did, he felt the presence of the darkness and knew it wanted to do bad things once he was alone with one of them. Then a voice of this real world came to him and he froze in terror at what it said.

"It's been a long time since I saw you, Erskine Chambers." Perhaps had he been sober, or had not been surrounded by these beautiful women, he could have ignored this comment and went on as though he hadn't heard it, act like he wasn't Chambers, but his eyes drifted around to the man who'd spoken, and he saw that he'd known this man once upon a time.

"Edwards," Olocher said.

"Long time no see," Edwards said, his ever-smiling face radiant. Olocher recalled him from their years in University together. What he could remember was Edwards was faithless, extremely manipulative, and not to be to be trusted if you were not entertaining to him. "What happened to your face?" he asked, still smiling.

"I was attacked and robbed," Olocher said, feeling the warmth of shame rise in his cheeks as some of the people in the room looked at him.

"How many times?" Edwards said then with a laugh and everyone else laughed too. The dark came over him like deep red and Olocher pushed the girl from his side and stood up. The girl protested but didn't retaliate. Olocher rushed for the door before he did something he would regret. Edwards was not a man to trifle with, he could feel that from him. No doubt he had members of the constabulary and army under his influence, and any assault on him could lead to a heavy prison sentence, or worse.

"Chambers!" Edwards called after him, "I was only joking!"

Once out on the street, Olocher walked with his head low, and his collars turned up to the icy wind. He didn't want to face the indignity of running away from that place, but that is exactly what he wanted to do.

"Chambers!" he heard Edwards call him and then hear the feet of his old acquaintance catch up.

"That's not my name anymore," Olocher said, turning to meet him.

"Your name is of no concern to me," Edwards said. "How have you been? What has you in this terrible city?"

Olocher thought for a moment and though Edwards seemed as sincere as could be, he wondered if it was possible word of his disinheritance had not spread to Edwards' ears by now.

"My father has cast me out and I've been tramping around, gambling and working the ships since then," he said bluntly. Edwards would not be prepared for him to tell the truth and it also meant Olocher wouldn't have to watch what he said as no lie would there waiting to trip him up. Edwards laughed out loud at this and slapped him on the shoulder.

"There always was a wild side to you, Chambers!" he said.

"I told you, I'm not Chambers anymore."

"What do you go by now, then?"

"Thomas Olocher."

"An odd name," Edwards said though thinking on it a moment and then dismissed it with a wave of his hand, "Let's have some drinks and catch up."

Edwards paid for the drinks, and Olocher entertained him with his story. He told all and true save the reason for leaving the convent and how that bloody darkness was still with him. Edwards listened with a serious face and asked questions here and there, but Olocher wondered was the darkness hidden or could this man see it in him. When he was finished talking, Edwards sat back and took in a deep breath.

"My, my, what a journey you've been on," he said. "What did you say the men who cut your face were known as?" he asked.

"The Cary Brothers," Olocher answered, a flash of hatred running through him. Edwards nodded and then called a bar boy over. He whispered something in the lad's ear and the boy ran off.

"Apologies for that," Edwards said, "Just something I forgot to do earlier." Then, going back to Olocher's story asked, "Did you ever run into them again? Or that Glamper fellow?"

"No, not yet anyway," Olocher said shaking his head, "For all I know they could be dead already."

They drank and talked some more, and then the boy came back and nodded to Edwards. He tossed the boy a coin — an amount that Olocher would have liked to see thrown his way any evening — and that was the end of that.

"Let's move on from here," Edwards suggested, and Olocher was happy to be led.

They walked a short time and Edwards checked the time when they had reached an open area in the back alleyway behind some large house. He stopped and looked seriously at Olocher.

"I'm going to meet someone here in a couple of minutes," he said. "Can you do me a favour and stand over there behind those crates until they come?"

"Are you looking for me to cover your back?" Olocher asked.

"Not at all, I've arranged this meeting for your benefit. I think you'll want to hear what these men have to say this evening."

"Who are they?"

"All in good time, Olocher," Edwards said. "Go behind those crates and keep quiet until it suits you; they should be here any minute."

Olocher couldn't really tell why he was following this introduction, but he did all the same and soon he heard the footsteps approaching down the alley.

Chapter 8

For a moment after hearing those footsteps, Olocher felt that he had wandered unwittingly into some kind of trap. He could picture Edwards nodding at the men as they arrived and then pointing to the cases where Olocher hid. He thought about fleeing, but decided against it. As it stood, he would have to pass them in the narrow alleyway, but if they dragged him out or forced him out into the open area, at least there was some room to move.

"Check around your feet, Olocher," he heard Edwards whisper then. He looked down and saw a wooden box, long and narrow. He bent and opened it, finding inside a long, hard wooden stick and a short dagger. What was Edwards up to? Whatever it was, Olocher felt it would be best for him to take up these arms against it.

"Gentlemen," Edwards said in a friendly greeting voice. "So good of you to come."

"Don't really have much choice, do we?" a man answered and at once Olocher knew he'd heard this voice before. But who did it belong to?

"There's always the choice, my good man," Edwards said. "You could disobey when I call for you and see what happens."

"We're here," another voice said, and this one Olocher recognised at once. "What do you want?" asked Trev of the Cary Brothers. Olocher felt his grip tighten around the hard stick and he had to hold himself back from going straight out there with it at the two men.

"There is someone I want you to meet; they will be along soon," Edwards said.

"Who?" Gary asked, a hint of nervousness in his voice.

"That is an excellent question," Edwards said and, in his mind, Olocher could see his annoying, smiling face. "I knew him as one man, but now he is another. I'd wager you boys never knew either of those names, or even his face."

"Enough of this," Trev said. "Who is it? When are they supposed to get here? We have something else we need to be attending to right now."

"You'll wait here until he comes, and that's the end of it!" Edwards snapped back at him. Olocher could hold himself in check no more.

Erupting from behind the crates, shouting a roar of anger, he smashed the stick down hard on Gary's head. There was a loud crack and a whiplash of blood splattered Olocher before Gary tumbled to the ground, dead. Trev didn't have a moment to react before the stick came up again, catching him under the jaw in the upswing. He reeled and then Olocher brought it down hard over his cheek. More bones broke and Trev toppled to the ground in dazed agony.

Olocher stopped now and was panting heavily.

"The dagger," he heard a voice say, and he couldn't be sure if it had been Edwards or the dark shape. Either way, he was too far gone and ready to listen. Leaning over, he took Trev by the ear and cut deeply into one cheek and then the other. The man wailed out in pain and then Olocher plunged the knife into his exposed throat. The cries turned to a gurgling sound as blood ran out of his mouth. Olocher let his head fall to the cobbles with a bang and then stood there looking down as the life ran out of the second man. Never in his life had he felt so powerful and alive. He savoured the moment, taking in every smell and twitch in his body. It was a few moments before he recalled where he was, and he suddenly remembered Edwards was there.He spun to face him, expecting a drawn sword to be in his hand, but Edwards just stood there looking at him.

"I thought you might want to let them know who you were first and scare them a little," he said, almost disappointed. "Instead you went crazy, and it was all over in a second."

"I'm sorry," was all Olocher's frazzled mind could think to say.

"No need to be sorry, Olocher, but I think you should leave here now. I'll get this mess sorted," he said nodding at the two men, "and if you see me again you act like we never met before, got it?" Olocher nodded, not really understanding what was going on. "You have started down a new path today, Olocher," Edwards said, smiling. "One that leaves Erskine Chambers in the past forever." Olocher nodded, feeling this exact thing. He was still looking down at the dead men, stunned. His only wish at this moment was that Glamper had have been there too.

"I have to say," Edwards said, "You didn't seem to savour their fear at all. When I seek revenge, I always make sure it is as enjoyable for me as possible."

What Edwards didn't understand, however, was that for Olocher this wasn't necessarily revenge; this had simply been the tipping point when the dark shape finally got what it wanted. He looked to Edwards and then walked away out of the alley without a word.

Chapter 9

Alderman James stood over the bodies of the two men in the alleyway.

"So these are the so-called Cary Brothers," he said. He took in the surrounding scene. One way in and one way out, high walls of the buildings on either side with few windows overlooking here. Some empty crates left either abandoned or stored. It looked to him as though one of two things had happened; either the brothers had been lured here and then killed, or more unlikely but not impossible, they had cornered someone here and got more than they expected.

The smaller of the two looked like he'd been felled with one blow and this led him to believe the men had been lured here, and perhaps it had been a surprise attack from behind the crates. The second man had taken more of a beating, but it had been the stab to the throat which had done for him. All in all, it must have been a quick affair and perhaps very little noise was made. The soldiers were asking questions in the buildings around, but James never held out too much hope for any answers. It seemed the people here were willing to let almost anything go unpunished rather than talk to the authorities.

Men like these die for all sorts of reasons, but in this case, James felt sure he could limit those reasons to two. There was anger involved here, perhaps even fury. This was either revenge, or the result of a double-cross. Philip Lee would be the man to get this information for James. Lee was a drunk and habitual thief who James had caught in the act some years ago. James let him go in exchange for general information from time to time as and when it was needed. Lee was happy to go along with this so long as James didn't approach him directly in the street where people would know what he was doing. Being known as a snitch, even if all he was doing really was gossiping, would not do him bodily health any favours around here.

James walked by the square later than afternoon and on seeing Lee hanging around in one of his usual spots, he tapped his cane twice on the ground as though trying to clear something from before walking on.

That evening, just after dark, lee arrived at the servant's entrance of James' house on Henrietta Street on the north side of the city.

"I don't like this, Alderman James," Lee said as soon as James appeared. "How long does this have to go on?"

"As long as I say it does," James said sternly, "Enough nonsense. Tell me what you know about the Cary Brothers's deaths last night."

"Not a lot as it happens," Lee said, "Lots of people are talking about it but no one has any news."

"What are they saying?"

"Only that brothers were at a card game in the Liberties when a message came for them and they left soon after."

"What was the message?"

"No one knows that, it was written down."

"Who delivered it?"

"A young boy."

"Who was this boy?" Lee shrugged at this.

"No one who was witness to it knew who he was. He could have been a bar boy or just some lad off the street; there's way of telling. People don't tend to take notice of these little fellas scurrying around delivering letters."

"What else?" James asked.

"Nothing, that's the whole of it. As far as anyone I know is concerned, the brothers weren't in any trouble with anyone at the moment."

"Well, someone didn't agree with that notion," James said.

"I suppose not," Lee agreed.

"Come back here tomorrow evening," James said, "I hope you will have more information on this by then." Lee looked crestfallen.

"I'm telling you; nobody knows anything!"

"Somebody knows something," James said, "and I intend to know it too!"

"I'll try, but I can't make any promises," Lee said, dejected.

"Where was the card game going on when they got the note?" James asked as Lee was about to walk away.

"The back of Devitt's," Lee answered, "Off Skippers Lane." James nodded.

The note or letter had not been on either of the dead men, so there was a chance they had left it behind at the tavern. If it wasn't still there, it was likely someone cleaning up had read it or someone at the game had seen who it was from. It was a start and all cases that had an end had to have one of those.

CHAPTER 10

Thomas Olocher slept late the morning after the events with the Cary Brothers. He'd come in as quietly as he could, hoping Paulina or her niece Mary would not hear him. There was no sound as he crept to his own room, so he thought he'd come in unheard. In his room, he lit a single small candle and then saw the blood on his hands and the sleeves of his coat. He went quickly to the basin stand in the corner and washed. The water was icy on this chilly night, and it stung his hands. He scrubbed at his fingers, watching the water turn a muddy colour as he did. When they were clean, he took the basin to the window to pitch it out, but stopped. In the dead of night, something like that would make an awful din and might give rise to questions. He put the bowl down by the window, deciding it best to cast it out in the morning when everyone else was doing the same thing.

He wrapped his coat up in itself with the bloody arms on the inside. He would have to get rid of that tomorrow, too. His first idea was that he could throw it into the river. He would decide in the morning. The thrill of the dark shape had overtaken him for a long time after the dazed confusion wore off, and he'd walked around for a long time before coming back to his lodgings. Olocher had been lucky not to have been picked up by the Parish Watch or the soldiers, he supposed. He was exhausted now, and all he wanted to do was sleep. He just hoped he was going to be able to. It was not something he needed to worry about. Only moments after lying down, he was fast asleep.

It was close to the afternoon when Olocher roused from his sleep. He got up and looked about. On seeing his bundled coat and then the dirty water, the events of the previous night came back to him with a force so strong he almost fell back onto the bed. A sudden nausea came over him and images of the open throat of Trevor Cary flooded his eyes like it was right there before him. He opened the window and took in a lungful of the cold air and then tossed the contents of the basin out into the laneway. The smell of the blood in the water prickled his nose and made him feel even more like vomiting.

The basin was rimmed from the sitting water all night, so he took his handkerchief and wiped at it until it no longer looked so bad. He would have to get more water to clean it better. The aroma of cooking came from the other rooms and Olocher heard the young Mary singing quietly to herself too. Hiding the basin under the bed until he could get it cleaned, he went out to the main room.

"Morning," he said to the aunt and niece.

"Just about," Paulina smiled at him. He smiled back. This woman had been growing on him since he moved in, and it was his desire to see her each day that kept him living here.

"What's in the pot?" he asked.

"Does it matter to a man who's been out half the night?" she answered playfully, and his smile broadened as he said,

"I suppose not." He sat at the table. Mary was looking at him from the other side of the room. He knew the little girl was afraid of him, so he didn't engage with her much.

"Go on, off and play in the bedroom, Mary," Paulina said as she dished up a bowl and placed it on the table for Olocher. Mary looked at first her aunt and then Olocher before getting up slowly and doing as she had been told.

When she was gone, Paulina said,

"There's been a lot of fuss this morning."

"How so?" he asked.

"A couple of thugs have been murdered," she said.

"Thugs?" Olocher felt his tongue going dry even saying this one word. Was this about what he'd done?

"The go about as the Cary Brothers," she went on. "They came from England, like yourself, a few years ago. Nothing but troublemakers from what I've ever heard of them."

"They're dead?" he asked, feeling the falseness of his voice and knowing for sure she would notice it too.

"Dead and gone and good riddance, if you ask me," Paulina said.

"Who killed them?"

"They don't know yet," she shrugged. "Or if they do, they're not saying."

"Does that kind of thing happen a lot around here?" he asked as conversationally as he could manage.

"Murder?" she asked, and he nodded. "Not all that often, but they're certainly not unheard of." There was a pause then as she ate a little and he thought about what he'd done. Edwards had done nothing to clean up the scene by the sound of things. What was he playing at? But the next sentence Paulina spoke made him feel a little happier about the situation. "When they do happen, though, it's rare that the person who did it gets caught," she said.

Chapter 11

Alderman James went to Devitt's tavern early in the day, knowing that it would be quieter then. The owner, a stocky man of gruff manner and deep set but twinkling blue eyes, greeted him warily as James entered the place. It was a very usual event.

"Alderman James," he said with a smile. "You're here to ask about the Cary Brothers, I expect?"

"Yes, Devitt," James said. "I'm not interested in anything else that goes on here, but I need to truth as it pertains to those two men." Devitt nodded at this, but James knew the tavern keeper would be careful with his words lest he slip about some illegal activities he thought James didn't already know about.

"What do you want to know?" Devitt asked, taking up a bottle and putting glass on the counter. He held the bottle up to ask James if you wanted a drink. James looked at it and shook his head.

"Anything you can tell me about the Cary Brothers," he said.

"Well," Devitt said, thinking. "They come in a bit, not a lot, but frequent enough, maybe once or twice a week."

"The same nights each week?"

"No," Devitt said after a pause.

"They come for card games?"

"Mostly."

"Do they often win?"

"Not as often as they lose," Devitt smiled.

"Did they owe anyone money? Significant money?"

"Not that I ever heard; they weren't extravagant gamblers. I never saw them in a high stakes game."

"Were you present when they got the note before leaving?"

"Yes, I was there for that."

"Did they look nervous about the note?"

"No, they looked a little put out, but I wouldn't say it was more than that."

"Did you see the note, what was written on it?"

"No," Devitt said, "But the girl cleaning up later saw it and told me what it said."

"Which was?"

"Meet me in the usual place."

"That's all? No signature or initial? A stamp or seal maybe?"

"No, I asked her the same thing, but she said no. I thought it odd too, but perhaps they knew the writing or maybe the boy told them who it was from?"

"Do you have the letter now?"

"No, she threw it in the fire while she was cleaning up."

"What about the boy? Did you recognise him?"

"Afraid not Alderman, all those young fellas look the same to me." James thought on Devitt's answers; he would talk to the girl who cleaned up later.

"Did they fight with anyone, either that night or any other recently?"

"No," Devitt said with certainty. "Actually, they were lying low for a good while. I think they were involved in something big, and they were keeping their noses clean in the lead up to it."

"Something big?"

"Yes, but I've no idea what."

James spoke to the girl who'd seen the letter and she could offer no more information than the employer had. He left feeling unsatisfied but happy with the knowledge the men seemed to know their killer and had regular meetings with him in the place they died.

Walking the short distance to the murder site, James stopped a few faces he recognised and asked some general questions about the recent activities of the brothers. They had nothing to say on the subject but when James asked if they had noticed a drop off in destructive behaviour of the men, a few nodded in agreement after thinking about it for a moment. Perhaps there was something to what Devitt has suspected. What could they have been planning? From what James knew of them, they did not seem like the planning kind. Whoever killed them knew them. He was sure of that. They were the real planner and killing those two brutes, most likely for what they already knew, was part of his plan all along.

James spoke to all the shopkeepers and tavern keepers whose premises looked out onto the entrance to the laneway the killings had taken place. Almost all had seen the brothers come and go into that alleyway frequently, but none of them ever saw anyone else with them. The meetings seemed to take place at any time of day, but there was no schedule to them that anyone noticed. It pained James to think how little these people noticed going on around them that was of actual importance. He had no doubt each man he spoke to could tell him who was having an affair or cheating his customers, but when it came to two known criminals meeting in a dead-end laneway, no one knew a thing or even ventured an opinion.

James didn't have the time to go ask at the houses that overlooked the laneway. He knew the soldiers would have already asked, but they would have only been concerned with the night of the murders. He would go there tomorrow and see if anyone knew anything. For now, evening was drawing in and Philip Lee would be at his door soon, hopefully with some new information.

Chapter 12

Olocher disposed of his bloodied coat by a quiet stretch of the river east of the market area. He'd weighted all the pockets with heavy stones, and watched it sink out of sight before he left. That was the afternoon after he'd killed the brothers. He was still in a strange state of both fear and euphoria, and he didn't know what to do with himself. It would have been good to talk to Edwards and see what was going on there, but he knew this would not be a good idea. Edwards had made it clear that they were not to know one another if they passed in the street, and he was well aware of the trouble his old university 'pal' could cause for him after what had happened.

With no better ideas coming to mind and restlessness getting the better of him, Olocher walked the city far and wide, exploring all points and only turning from one course when he saw that if he kept on going he would leave the city. It wasn't a big city, but there were so many streets, alleys, and passageways it was like a vast maze.

After two days of this, Thomas Olocher found himself back in the Whiskey Cabin in which he'd gotten the directions to Hell. The cabin keeper nodded in greeting when he came in, and Olocher ordered a jug. The place was filling up around him even as he stood there, and it made him realise the time. A lot of the trades would shut up about now and these were those people coming in now to unwind a little (or a lot) after a hard-working day.

Olocher took a table near the back before it got too busy; he had an idea he would be here for a while tonight and he didn't want to spend any more time on his feet after all his tramping of late. The drink was excellent going into him and he felt calmer as it took hold of his senses. He was glad that the talk of the people had moved on from the murders to some scandal involving some Lord or other. The atmosphere of the place was warm and jovial.

Olocher watched the people as they laughed and joked, and it felt good to be in their company. Now and then someone would sit by him and talk to him a minute or two about any random thing that popped into their heads and then move on, a new acquaintance made. Over by the window an enormous man, the look of a blacksmith on him, and his smaller friend put away jugs at a steady rate. Olocher made eye contact with the smaller of the two men, striking pale blue eyes he had, and when the blacksmith left for home, the man came over and sat opposite Olocher.

"Cleaves," he said, holding out his hand.

"Olocher." They shook.

"I haven't seen you in here before," Cleaves said, smiling.

"I'm new enough to the place," Olocher replied. Cleaves nodded.

"I hear the accent," he said. "London?"

"Close by," Olocher agreed.

"You left London for here?" Cleaves smiled with a look of incredulity on his face.

"It wasn't much of a choice," Olocher said, also smiling. He was trying to sound mysterious, but he felt a pang at suddenly knowing what he'd said was true.

"That what happened to your face?" Cleaves asked, running lines down his own cheeks as he said it. Olocher nodded. He barely thought about his scars anymore, didn't even see them in his reflection all that often, but he was never allowed to forget them for more than a few days at a time. Someone would always ask him what had happened. He never told the truth, and each time, it was a little different. This man, Cleaves, however, only nodded and didn't ask anymore.

They spoke and drank for a time and then discovered a shared history of being in Bristol. Cleaves had been there only a short time, but he knew some places Olocher spoke of and he even knew who Glamper was. They were the last two in the cabin at closing time.

Out in the street, they said their goodbyes, knowing they would run into one another again in the cabin soon enough. Cleaves went one way and Olocher the other. He was happy and drunk and as he walked on the cold street, lust came over him. It was a pleasant feeling, and his eyes looked about for a streetwalker. He had money on him, and it would be a good finish to his enjoyable evening.

He only had to walk one street before meeting a girl out for business. They agreed on a price and Olocher paid her upfront. She looked around and then led him into a dark passageway between some housing buildings.

"We have to be quiet in here," she whispered, pointing up to the windows above. He nodded. As they went further into the darkness, a change came over him, and his lust ebbed dramatically. At first, it disappointed him, but then, as the new desire made itself known to him, great joy overcame him once more. It was dark enough now that he could only make out the bare outline of her, but he could see her, and right now that was all that was important. He drew his knife.

CHAPTER 13

James found himself once more standing over a body in a closed off area behind some houses. This time, it was a prostitute called Mandy Tavers. Even though it was daylight now, the sun didn't reach too far into this passageway. It felt oppressive and the smell of the blood and viscera was thick in the air. This woman had been savagely attacked, ripped up with most likely a dagger. He couldn't count how many lacerations there were to her skin at a cursory look, but he knew the number would be very high, much higher than anything else he'd ever seen before.

Mandy's eyes were still open when he arrived, and even though dead, James felt he could see the fear in them. He tried to piece together what had happened, and it looked fairly clear. Someone had approached her for business. They had come down here away from the street with her leading the way and then at this point she turned to him and he attacked and killed her very violently. It was unlikely in James's opinion that there was any motive for this crime. The man wanted to kill, and Mandy was in the wrong place at the wrong time.

He noticed that they had stabbed the woman through the throat and this made him think of the second of the Cary Brothers's to be killed a few nights back. That too had taken place in a closed off area, though larger than this one. Was it possible this was the work of the same person? It made little sense that it would be, but there were a couple of consistencies and he had a feeling in his gut he knew better than to ignore.

As he thought more about this, James also linked the killing of the first brother. That had been a forceful blow to the skull, a single hit that had killed him. Could that have been like the fury seen here? Only the weapon was different and the man went down faster than the assailant would have liked? Possibly, he thought, nothing to rule it out, anyway.

This time, people had heard the murder as it happened, and few people had looked out their window. In the darkness, however, they could only make out the shape of the man running away and nothing they described would make the man stand out in any way. He already knew it was a man who did this, so in effect, it was tantamount to nothing, save the direction the man ran away.

It had been the same with Lee's second visit. No new information had been forthcoming, and no one seemed to know what the Cary Brothers were working on. They were only in the city about a year and were still trying to make a real name for themselves. If they got on the wrong side of the wrong people, it wasn't public knowledge.

As he was leaving the scene feeling he could learn nothing more from it today. James saw an elderly man whom he'd questioned in the houses about the Cary Brothers deaths, across the street stop and squint as though to see him better. When the old man seemed sure he was looking at who he thought he was looking at, he motioned for James to follow him before slipping into a coffeehouse. James looked around to see if anyone near him had been the intended receiver of this message. It seemed that he was, and he walked over and went inside out of the cold.

The old man, Jeffers, the name came back to James, was sitting on a comfortable-looking sofa waiting for his coffee.

James didn't look to the counter though he wanted one now, but went straight to him.

"You were looking for me to come with you?" he asked.

"Yes," Jeffers said, looking around, "Please, sit down, Alderman. I have ordered a coffee for you."

This was a surprise, but a welcome one, and James sat. It was good to get off his feet. As though on cue, the waiter arrived with the steaming drink, set them down, and left.

"Thank you," James said, taking up his cup.

"Think nothing of it," Jeffers said. They both sipped.

"You have something to tell me?" James asked. Jeffers nodded, coffee still in his mouth unswallowed. A noisy gulp as it went down.

"I didn't want to say back at the house," he started, "But I heard the commotion out the back when the two lads were killed."

"What did you hear?" James said, interested but also annoyed that this information was only coming to him now.

"I heard the shout of the man who killed them."

"What did he shout?"

"It wasn't words, just a roar," Jeffers said, nodding as though hearing it now.

"A roar?" James said, "Of anger, perhaps?"

"Oh definitely," Jeffers answered, "This was like anger and pain wrapped up in one, like it had been a long time burning up inside the man before it was released." This was the most descriptive thing anyone had ever said to James in relation to a sound, and it made all the difference to him. Revenge sprang into his mind.

"Did you see the attacker?" he asked.

"Just as he left, the murders were out of my scope for seeing."

"Did you see his face?"

"Not like you'd have wanted me to," Jeffers said apologetically, "But from the side, I wouldn't be able to know him if I saw him again, but I thought there was something odd about his face, like he had something on it a mask, maybe?"

"Odd in what way?"

"Well, it didn't look like a mask, but there were ridges on his face that shouldn't be there in a side look like that." James nodded, noting this down.

"What was he wearing?"

"Couldn't say, black coat maybe?"

"Was he alone?"

"I don't think so," Jeffers said, but here he looked puzzled.

"Why?"

"I thought I heard him talking to someone a moment, but I looked for a long time and didn't see anyone else leaving the laneway." James knew there was only one way in and out of that laneway. He didn't press Jeffers on this anymore, as it was clear this was all he knew. Perhaps the killer had been talking to himself, or maybe some parting words for the dead men? Either way, revenge had raised in his mind. An intuition he would follow up as best he could.

CHAPTER 14

Thomas Olocher lay in his room, looking up at the ceiling. His legs throbbed, and he ran his hands lightly over his damaged thighs. His right thigh bore some bruising, but it was the four slash marks there that caused the most pain. His left thigh was more heavily bruised and felt dead and numb. Neither leg was a pleasure to put any weight on. After he'd killed the prostitute, who he now knew was called Mandy, Olocher had rushed away from the scene still very heavily under the influence of the dark shadow. He was very close to being back in his apartment when he saw the bloody rags of his right trouser leg. Only then did he feel the pain, and the very pronounced limp came on him.

He staggered on, knowing he had to get off the streets before he was seen. He stopped for a moment in the stairwell of building he rented in, a thin flickering of candle still left on. Olocher felt his legs through the holes and sticky blood met him along with the ringing pain. Using the rest of his trouser leg and despite the agony it caused him, Olocher wiped up the blood and held the holes together so as not to let blood drip all over the stairs as he went up.

Once in his room, he bundled the trousers off, holding his breath and mouth closed so not to cry out in pain, and wrapped them in the shirt he'd been wearing this evening. He got the water jug and washed his cuts. They were down into the flesh, but he was able to stem the blood fast enough. He was very surprised that he had no memory of cutting himself like this. It looked like it would have been excruciating. When he was finished washing, he ripped up another shirt and made a bandage for his cut thigh. He sat there looking at the dirty bloody water and recalled being in a similar position not too long ago and....

The bowl. The night he killed the Cary Brothers he'd washed their blood in this same bowl but hadn't been able to throw the water out until morning. There had been a line of scum around the inside of the bowl, and he'd hidden it under the bed until he could clean it. Only now, he remembered he'd never cleaned it, and yet here it was in its usual spot, and it had been cleaned before he started washing this evening. Paulina must have found it and washed it for him.

That was careless, he thought. That was the kind of thing that could get you caught. He wondered if there was any way she would have known what it had been. Surely not. She would have made a serious fuss about it if she had. Still, it was a possibility. The dark shape was growing again, but Olocher pushed it away. He liked Paulina, had indeed developed both a fondness and a lust for her simultaneously. He wouldn't do anything to hurt her.

Despite the hour, Thomas Olocher tossed the water out into the laneway, pulling back inside the window and closing it as fast as he could so no one hearing it would know where it came from. It made a terrific noise in the frosty night and someone let out a shout of annoyance at having their sleep disturbed. He cleaned the bowl with the remainder of the shirt he'd used for a bandage. He couldn't leave these things to chance anymore. If he didn't rein himself in, he'd be facing the gallows in a matter of weeks.

To his credit, Olocher did a fine job of reining himself in. After disposing of the clothes the next day, he rested up, thinking about what he could do to occupy his days in the future. His aim now was to work so that at night, when the darkness seemed most powerful in him, he would be too tired to accommodate it. He didn't fool himself into thinking he'd killed for the last time. No, he knew there would be more. He'd just decided he was going to do his best to make them as infrequent as possible in the name of self-preservation.

The work he came upon was down by the market, loading and unloading the ships that came in. It was hard work, thankless and not well paid. What it did, however, was to tax his body and make him tired in the evenings. He'd not worked so hard since his first sea voyage and his body had become a little softer than before in his gambling and cheating run. Now he was hardening up again, getting stronger, and before long (and before he knew it himself) he wasn't so tired at the end of his shifts. He could go with some of the others to the taverns after work and this return to drinking also saw the rejuvenation of the dark shape.

One night, after a heavy drinking binge with some of his fellow workers, a fight broke out. Olocher would not recall what it was about, or much about the fight itself, for that matter, until he was told a few days later. It seemed that the other man started the fight, but Olocher had escalated it beyond all reason very quickly and had to be pulled off the man before he killed him. The man who told Olocher about the fight laughed at his not remembering it, saying Olocher had swung both hands in constant motion like a maniac and had even hit his own legs many times in the melee.

Perhaps this was a way to sate the monster in future, he thought. It certainly enjoyed the fight, and the pain caused to the other man and if Olocher was careful to only fight when he knew there was someone there who would pull him off before things got too bad, that might be the best of both worlds. The more he thought about this, the better an idea he found it to be. He smiled as he went back to work.

Chapter 15

Some time passed as Thomas Olocher worked this job by the docks. Many weeks went by without so much as a word uttered in anger from his lips. The darkness slept as the last week of November came around. It was bitterly cold by the river and his hands hurt with the work. Olocher wasn't alone in this and many a man came off his work grumpy as a result. The men would drink in the cabins and taverns then and their sore hands would ache even as they lifted a drink. It could only be a matter of time before Olocher was back fighting again.

He was drinking more now and as a result, his fighting increased too. Fighting was so common within and outside any of the drinking houses that the soldiers rarely bothered to do anything about it, even if they happened to be passing as a donnybrook was taking place in the streets. Olocher revelled in this, or more accurately, the part of Olocher that lived for violence and the pain and suffering of others did.

One evening in mid-December, Olocher was on his way home. There had been no trouble this night, and he was happy enough with that. He felt all the fighting was taking a toll on him (he didn't consider for a moment that it might have been all the drink he took on of late). He would prefer for a few weeks where nothing happened, and he might have a chance to recover some.

Then a streetwalker made the unfortunate mistake of approaching him as he passed.

"Hello, lovely," she said sweetly as she took hold of his arm. Olocher turned to look at her and as he did, she saw his scarred face and recoiled, pulling her hand away from him. In his state, this was enough for the dark to come to the surface at once, fuelled by his anger at her rejection of him. He swung a large hand around and punched her in the face. She went reeling against the wall of the building behind her, completely taken by surprise. She was so dazed with the blow she didn't even call out before he pounced on her, knocking her to ground. He sat astride her pummelling hard with both hands, not even noticing when she lost consciousness.

The noise came to him; he heard the thud of his fits on her and some on his own legs and he felt the pain he was causing himself. An image of the knife came to mind, and he paused long enough to reach down for it. This would be the last time this little bitch ever insulted Thomas Olocher!

That was when the voice called out a loud,

"Oi, what are you doing to that girl!" Olocher took control of his body and he got up and ran without ever looking in the direction the voice came from.

"Stop!" it called out, "Murder!" but Olocher could tell that the man wasn't chasing him. The voice was getting farther away.

That night, Olocher did not stop running until he was back at home. He went up to the apartment and slipped into his room and lay on the bed. His heart pounded and his head ached from the exertion. That had been too close.

"What were you thinking?" he whispered harshly, "In the middle of the street!" he said to himself. But he knew it wasn't really himself he was talking to. He also knew that the woman from tonight was not dead. If she could talk, she might be able to describe him. This was not good, and he didn't see a way of getting to her to finish off the job.

Something else was nagging at him and he also knew what this was. The creature within had not been satisfied. Nearly dead this time was not enough. It would pull and paw at Olocher's soul now until it killed again. This time it would have to be done with purpose, late at night and somewhere dark enough he would not be seen. A street walker would always fit the bill, but he would have to go farther afield for this one, somewhere over on the north side of the river.

This is exactly what he did, only three nights later. Everything down to the last moment had come semblance of a plan to it. He found the woman, let her choose the dark spot, and then finally let the darkness take over when everything was in place.

When it was over, the woman dead and having not made a sound, Olocher had even had the forethought to leave spare clothes by the river in the same place he'd dumped the coat before. He sat by the water and cleaned his own gnarled and scarred thighs, fresh cuts there now but the pain no longer irritating to him but a shrill reminder of what he'd just done and hence something pleasurable to him now.

When he got home that evening, he wasn't rushing, wasn't panicked. His clothes and body were clean, and he got into bed and slept soundly for the first time in many months.

CHAPTER 16

Alderman James looked at the map of the city on his study wall. In it he had placed pins that designated the murder sites of the Cary Brothers, two prostitutes and the attack site of another prostitute. Having been to all three prostitute attack sites, he knew the same man had committed them, and his instinct was telling him the first two murders of the brother's was part of it too. James couldn't link them up, though; in fact, didn't think he ever would. He thought the brothers' murders had been an aberration in this man's plans. He'd wanted revenge on those men, plain and simple — and he'd gotten it. But the women's attacks were different. They were much more primitive and violent. This was a sick person, to be sure.

James also knew the direction in which the attacker had fled on three of the occasions. Though this didn't necessarily mean the man lived in the directions indicated, James felt he did. And now that he'd been able to talk to Stella Ryan, the woman who was attacked and lived, there was something more important too. The man's face was scarred across his cheek.

What Jeffers had seen wasn't a mask, but the lifted flesh of the man's scarred cheek, and from the direction Jeffers had seen the man and Stella's story, James also knew it was on the man's right cheek. It was true that there was no shortage of men in this city with scars on their faces, but it certainly limited the pool of suspects for now.

Speaking to Stella had been hard; she was not long awake when James came to her. After a few days of unconsciousness, she was still groggy and very much traumatised and afraid by what had happened to her. She was in bed when he came to her and he was shocked by her appearance. Never before had he seen a face puffed a swelled in the way hers was. Her eyes and mouth were deep in the flesh and her nose broken badly. Deep bruising covered her skin on both her face and the flesh of her arm that he could see. It was a miracle this woman was alive, though James felt sure she would have preferred not to be considering her current state. He didn't see too much recovery from this, and she certainly wouldn't be able to work her old profession anymore.

Stella told him what happened, what she could recall anyway, and James listened. It delighted him to hear of the scar, and this made sense of what Jeffers saw, too.

"He said nothing to you at all?" James asked hopefully.

"No, he just turned on me straight away," she said as fresh tears peeped out of her eyes. This was a pity. It would have good to be able to put an accent on the man, help narrow the field down even further. Jeffers hadn't been able to place any accent on the man, either.

Looking at the map again in his study, days after talking to Stella, he noticed something else in the lines. The latest murder was very far away from the others. So far that it might be easily thought a different suspect. James imagined this had been the design of the killer. He was becoming more careful, and it was possible that from now on, there would be no evidence at all to go on.

The killings had started off by chance in a way, and then he went a little heavy in his desire for more. That he killed so soon after the attack on Stella showed James that this was deep inside the man, that he had to kill or else it would drive him mad.

This man wasn't stupid, however. He knew how close he'd come to being caught. That was why he went so far to kill this last time, and why the killings may become either more widespread or less frequent now. He knew he had to be more careful, and that made James' job even more difficult.

Up to now, it had been more impetuous on the killer's behalf and he had probably made all the mistakes he was going to by now. The evidence to catch the man was already out there, James was sure of it. He just had to find out what that was.

The map showed him one avenue of investigation. The direction the man left the scene each time he'd been seen narrowed his living area to the south-east of the city. It was still a large area, but it cut the city down by four-fifths. If he was correct in this; it was only a matter of time before this man hung for what he'd done.

CHAPTER 17

The constant drinking had become too much for her. Olocher supposed it was understandable, but he still didn't like it. Paulina wanted him to look for somewhere else to live. She was timid but firm; she couldn't have her niece growing up with his current behaviour in the apartment.

"She's getting older, now," Paulina said, "Getting to that impressionable age." Olocher nodded, though he didn't quite know what she meant by this.

"You'll let me stay until I find something else?" he asked.

"Of course, Thomas. I've no desire to see you stuck for a roof over your head. It's just not suitable for you to be here long term anymore. I'm very sorry about this." He could hear the sincerity in her voice, and he felt ashamed that he'd led her to this decision. All the time he'd been drinking and fighting, he'd been thinking of only the darkness and never once did he consider how he might seem to those he shared a home with.

"I can only thank you for taking me in when you did," he said glumly. "I've been happy here and will be sad to leave."

"I'm sad about it too," she said, taking hold of his hand on the table and giving it a quick squeeze before letting go. "But it's for the best."

"Alright," Olocher said; her touch had stung him, a feeling he'd never experienced before. He wanted to take her hand in his once more and just hold it, feeling its softness and warmth against his skin. These feelings for Paulina, a desire that wasn't lust but somehow emotional, had come over him from time to time in the past and he never knew what to do about it. Now that their hands had been in contact, this feeling came over him with more force than ever and it hurt his heart to think that he was soon to be leaving her. He stood up and left the room without looking at her; he didn't think he could bear it.

As it often the case with men who are their own worst enemies, Olocher decided that as he was getting put out of his home because of his drinking, the best thing he could do right now would be to go to the tavern and drown his sorrows.

On his way, Olocher thought about his future for the first time in a long while. It wouldn't be so hard to get somewhere else to say — he always heard people advertising rooms no matter where he went. The trick would be to find somewhere he could come and go at his pleasure, with the least number of eyes on his movements. He thought of perhaps somewhere that overlooked the river on one side, somewhere that was unlikely to be so much observed.

"Looking glum, Olocher," a cheerful voice said. Olocher looked up and saw Cleaves standing before him.

"Oh, hello," he replied "Just deep in thought."

"Nothing too immoral, I hope!" Cleaves said with a wink. Olocher smiled back,

"No, not at all. It seems I have to find somewhere else to live."

"Getting kicked out?"

"Something like that."

"Don't worry, there are a ton of places in your neighbourhood that will take you in," Cleaves said. Olocher nodded,

"I'm going to the cabin; do you fancy a drink?"

"It's a little early," Cleaves said. "But why not!"

There was no one else in the Whiskey Cabin when they got there, and the barman looked happy to see someone in. They took a jug each and sat in the seat closest to the window to be able to see the busy street outside. It was still the light of afternoon in late January, but the evening would come soon. As they looked out, Olocher saw thin snowflakes begin to fall.

"It's snowing," he said in surprise. Cleaves looked out and nodded.

"That's been coming a while, now," he said.

"What does Dublin look like covered in snow?" Olocher asked.

"Beautiful," Cleaves answered, still looking outside. "Just beautiful."

They drank the evening away, and the cabin filled up. The heat of the bodies making it a warm comfortable place against the cold outside. Olocher asked about and before going back to Paulina's that night he had four potential leads on a place to stay.

On his walk home, he realised it would not be too much longer before he'd be making a new trek. It saddened him, and in this vulnerable state, the dark shape tried to reassert itself. Olocher had been in a couple of fights of late, but hadn't come close to killing anyone. The shape didn't like this and wanted fresh blood. Thomas Olocher looked to the ground as he walked, not wanting to play any part in someone's death tonight. He was going home for one of the last times and he wanted to be able to savour it when he got there.

Someone spoke to him, but he kept on walking without looking. He didn't hear the words until he was farther on down the street, but he knew then it had been a streetwalker. Were they ever going to learn? On any other night, that could have been the last mistake that woman ever made. Then he told himself, what else can they do? They have to be out on the street, and they have to talk to people to earn money. Men walking alone are the most likely of targets for them, the ones most likely to be looking for those of their trade.

When he got in, Olocher was as quiet as possible. He took in the room, the still warm though extinct fire, the smell of the cooking pot from earlier in the day. How he'd liked this place without ever really knowing or appreciating this fact. It was such a shame he was going to miss it. If only that little girl Mary hadn't come here to live, thing would be different. He scoured his memory, trying to recall if Paulina had ever told him why Mary lived with her. He supposed her parents must have passed away, but he didn't remember hearing this.

Lying in bed, he looked up at the ceiling and thought of Paulina. How different might things have been if Mary had not come? Or would they be any different at all? It was hard to tell, and even harder to know.

CHAPTER 18

The day of his moving out was not long in coming around. In early February, Thomas Olocher left the house and moved to another room in the area known as Hell. He now roomed with an old man, hard of hearing and not much interested in what Olocher got up to at all. The man was called Tymon, and he worked in leather and drank cheap spirits when he wasn't working. He cooked a stew pot every few days and reheated it as he needed, and encouraged Olocher to do the same.

The bed Olocher slept in was uncomfortable and the room drafty and cold. It was a big step down from what he'd had, but he supposed he was getting what he paid for. Nowhere else had the bonus of a drunken house partner who didn't give a damn what you did.

In a way, Olocher had known that living here was giving license to his dark accompaniment to roam more freely. He'd agreed to live with Tymon in a moment of sadness when he knew the shadow was in part control.

One night as Olocher sat by the fire, Tymon came in with skinful on him and started drinking again. When his stories got to be too much for him, Olocher said he was going out and he left the old man to his memories. Olocher was angry at his quiet evening being disturbed and he knew this would never have happened back at Paulina's. Even as he walked out the door onto the street that night, he knew he was going to kill again before he returned.

He wasn't sure when exactly he'd stopped thinking about Paulina that evening and started looking for a victim. It was still early in the night when he had his first altercation. Olocher wasn't drunk by now, but he had been to two taverns already. A man walked into him coming from a coffeehouse as Olocher passed. The man apologized good naturedly and took Olocher by the coat to dust him off in a friendly gesture. Olocher saw red and grabbed the man's wrists and smashed his forehead into the wide-eyed face that greeted this surprise grab. The thud was sickening, and the man called out in pain before falling back and clothing both hands to his face. Olocher saw the blood trickle between the man's fingers, but he didn't follow up with an attack. There were too many people around. He rushed off into the night.

Later, close to midnight, he fought briefly with a sailor who'd said something derogatory about him. This time he launched savagely at the man and it had been hard not to take his knives out. (He'd taken to strapping to knives to his thighs and making holes in his pockets so he could get to them easily if he needed). No one pulled him off the man this time, but one of the other sailors joined in and this led to a regular tavern brawl with about ten men involved before it was over. Amid this, someone had knocked over Olocher and he looked on a moment at what was happening and then thought it best that he left. There was no doubt that the army would be along soon to deal with this one.

Now it came to the real purpose of the night. Olocher was tired and felt he should pick someone quickly to get it over with. The Darkness didn't like this, however, and he ended up walking the streets for an hour before he saw what he wanted. He was about to approach her when another man appeared and engaged with her. They agreed on a price and she led him down a laneway just a little up the street.

This and the idea that he would have to go looking again for someone else that suited the taste annoyed Olocher. Then a voice came to him, sounding very much like his own.

"Why don't you go down that laneway and do both of them?"

"Who not, indeed," he answered. Casting a quick glance up and down the road for witnesses, and seeing none, he walked over and entered the laneway after the pair.

Olocher expected to find them in the act by now, but it seemed they were arguing as he got closer to them. The man was trying to negotiate on the price once more. They were speaking in a rough whisper as Olocher crept towards them, using the darker side of the laneway to mask his approach.

Coming close now, he took the knives from his thighs and held on in each hand. He gripped them tightly, thinking what way he should do this. Was it more prudent to take the man down quickly, in the throat, say, or would it be better to knock the woman over as he dealt with the man? In the end, as ever, Thomas Olocher didn't get to decide. He was too close to it now, and the dark shape took over.

He pounced forward in silence, both hands flailing with sharpened blades, and took them both on in one attack. He would remember later seeing frightened eyes, blood flowing from cheeks. All three of them hit the ground hard, and Olocher continued with the knives. He was only barely aware that the man had scrambled just out of reach. He was on his feet then and running. Olocher would never see him again.

The woman was not so lucky, and the man didn't call out for help. He fled for his own skin and left her to her fate. A gruesome and horrible fate that would shock even Alderman James when he came to the site the following morning.

CHAPTER 19

Though he wouldn't know for a time yet, Alderman James had already looked into the place the killer was currently staying. James had talked to Tymon back in early January and it had been fruitless, as he hadn't even met the man with the scarred face at that point.

It had been a frustrating search thus far. As expected, there had been no shortage of men with scars on their cheek but each one so far had an alibi for at least some of the murders. All of this interviewing and following up took so much time, and James had other tasks to complete at the same time and court cases to attend in his role. It was taking days to complete each street in the areas he'd narrowed his search to.

This latest murder, though he'd expected it sooner, was the most gruesome so far. Blood was splattered all over the ground and walls, and the killer himself must have been covered in it, too. There was no way this woman was ever going to be recognised by her face. Her throat was a gaping ragged hole, and her chest was riddled with stab and slash marks. It was such a terrible scene James had to wonder if there was any blood left inside the body at all.

People had heard this crime taking place, heard the woman screaming briefly, but no one had come to her aid. The people here were frightened and cowered from the windows in case the killer saw them look out and come for them next. It was frustrating in the extreme all the witnesses there could have been.

While he was about, James looked in on the tavern where the brawl had taken place. He asked how it started and the tavern keeper told him at first it had been two men, a man with a scar on both cheeks and a sailor, but that it had turned into something bigger. James jumped on this,

"The man with the scars," he said, "Do you know him?"

"He's been in before, but I don't know his name."

"Who does he talk to?"

"He never spoke to anyone the couple of times he was here, save me when he wanted a drink."

"And what did he drink?"

"Whiskey."

"Each time?"

"Yes, as I can remember anyway."

James thanked him and moved on. He was heading back to Hell to continue his door-to-door questioning, when a man with a bandaged face came up to him.

"Alderman James," he said, "Please?" James stopped and looked at the man's two black eyes and puffy face.

"Yes?" he said.

"Something has to be done," the man said, "I came out of that coffeehouse last night only to be assaulted by some lunatic!"

"He did this to your face?" James asked.

"Yes, I have spoken to the soldiers, but they say this kind of thing happens every day and it is unlikely anything will come of their searching." Something made James ask the,

"Did you see this man's face?"

"Yes, quite clearly," the man answered, "A gruesome fellow."

"Scars on his face?"

"Yes, both sides of his face, like something from a nightmare." James nodded.

"Which way did he leave you?"

"That way," the man pointed. James looked behind him the way he'd come.

"I'll look into this," James said, and he continued on his way.

So, it seemed that this man was on something of a mini rampage last night before killing. James smiled and the knowledge he'd gained today. Men with scars on their faces were common, but men with scars on both cheeks were not so common. This whittled the pool of suspects down once more.

James went to his trusted source on these matters. Philip Lee was not at his usual post when James got there, but a few minutes later they practically ran into one another on a street corner. James glanced around quickly and then whispered to Lee,

"Come this evening, tell me about everyone you can find out about who had scars on both cheeks." Lee looked at him in surprise and then nodded quickly before walking on without saying a word. James knew it would annoy him that people might have seen them talking, but there were much bigger issues at stake here than Philip Lee's reputation.

What Alderman James didn't know, and would never know, was that Philip Lee was not the only person to hear this request for information. Only feet away, with his back turned to the street and looking in the window of a clothes shop, was the very man with scars on his face. He didn't move and let James pass by him, preoccupied with his own thoughts. Then the man looked back up the street at the departing Lee. He knew this man, to see at least, and that meant he in turn, probably knew Olocher. Something would have to be done.

Chapter 20

Thomas Olocher spent the rest of that afternoon following and noting what Philip Lee did. He seemed to know everyone about. In every tavern, coffeehouse, market stall or traders he went to, he spoke to people in the manner of an acquaintance. There was no doubt some of the people he spoke to would have been able to point the finger in Olocher's direction. He was known well enough himself in some places. Well enough that the information would get back to Alderman James this evening if Olocher would allow it.

The dim of late afternoon was settling when Lee left the area. He headed south first and then doubled back some streets over to head north. No doubt this was his way of covering up some of the facts about where he was going. It wouldn't do if people knew he was an informant for the Alderman. How many people would vie for his blood If that was public knowledge?

Olocher was happy now as all day Lee had been amongst people and now he would have no choice but to travel alone. Olocher didn't know where the Alderman lived, but he was sure it was in one of the richer streets close to the river's far bank. Drawing closer to Lee, he hoped soon to see him slip into some alleyway as a shortcut. If he did that, Olocher would be up behind him as fast as he could with blades drawn.

To his disappointment, however, Lee continued along the principal streets until he came to Henrietta Street. As he walked past one house, Olocher saw Lee look at the door and windows, and he knew at once this was James' house. "He's going to go around to the servant's entrance," Olocher whispered. Knowing this, he crossed the road and ran on ahead to overtake Lee. He didn't look across the road at his intended victim, but simply jogged on and went off ahead and around the corner. He would have looked in this now falling darkness like any servant rushing back to his master's home from some errand.

Olocher entered the laneway that would lead to the back of James' house and waited in the first alcove he could find. He took out his knives and waited, doing his best to breathe into the wall and down towards the ground to disguise the mist of his breaths. When he heard footsteps in the alley a few moments later, he knew the time had come. He stopped breathing as Lee came closer.

There was no let-up in the footsteps and Olocher could tell Lee was as comfortable walking up this way as he'd ever been in the past. The steps drew level with his position. At first, all Olocher could see were the wide eyes of Lee as he lunged at him. The recognition and fear of the scars were clear in this face and so was the knowledge of his own death.

The snitch didn't have time to say or scream anything before both blades slashed at his throat in quick succession. Blood flowed out and down his chest. Lee looked at Olocher a moment with what looked like a questioning face and then fell to his knees. With the self-preservation part over, the darkness took over and the wall and laneway were soon stained with blood.

Thomas Olocher left the scene, his clothes, face, and hands a glorious red mess, but he didn't rush. He was on another of those magnificent highs that often accompanied his murders. If anyone stopped of challenged him, he was ready to kill again no matter where it was or how many people were around. His legs took him back towards the river and he slowly got back to himself.

The rush wore off, and he felt exhausted all at once. As he reached the bridge, he realised what kind of state he was in and how unlikely he was to get home without being noticed. It was still early enough, and men would fill the bars of the less well-off south side about now.

Despite the coldness of the night, he took off his coat, tossed it into the Liffey and then launched himself into the depths behind it. He rose back to the surface with his body going numb from the shock of the cold. His coat floated off downriver and away from him and he let it go. He made for the south bank near and wiped his face and hands clean as he went.

When he got out, a couple of sailors looked oddly at him. Olocher was too cold to care about this or challenge them and he just stumbled on back towards his lodgings. He could think only of the fire, dry clothes and then his bed. It had been foolish to jump into the river and he could only hope now that he did not develop a serious cold. Although if he did, he might have to stay in bed for a few days and that would take care of his need to lie low now that he had killed again. Tymon would sort him out with a bottle of brandy and some stew if he were bedridden. He was sure of that.

Later that evening, as Olocher sat in front of the fire in the fresh clothes, new thoughts came to him. James was on to him. He might not know who he was just yet, but that was only a matter of time. James knew about the two scars on his face and that would be enough. Olocher was going to have to leave the city, and soon. He would have to think about where he was going to go and how he was going to get there. This thought led him to think of Paulina and he imagined asking her to leave with him, to set up with him somewhere else. He wouldn't tell her about the reason for his leaving, of course. But he wished she could come with him, even it meant bringing her little niece, Mary Sommers.

He thought of Galway and the three of them living in a tiny house. The idea was as pleasant as the fire that warmed his body.

CHAPTER 21

Alderman James knocked on the fateful door. So far, no one else had answered in this building, but he heard at once someone was coming to this one. A woman answered, and she looked worried when she saw who it was.

"What's the matter?" she asked with terror in her eyes.

"Don't be alarmed, Madam," James said as pleasantly as he could, "I'm knocking on all doors in the neighbourhood asking a few questions in relation to the murders you have no doubt heard about."

"Murder?" Paulina asked. James ignored this, knowing she was still only getting past her shock of seeing him at her door.

"Are there any men living under your roof?" he asked. Paulina shook her head and James was about to move on with his other general questions when she said,

"There was until recently, though."

"Who was that?"

"His name was Olocher," she said. "Thomas Olocher."

"How long did he live here?"

"Only about nine months," Paulina said. "He got to be too much in the end, and I had to ask him to move out." James raised his eyebrows at this.

"Oh yes, in what way?" he asked.

"Drinking too much, and a lot of fighting."

"Fighting?"

"Yes, but not here, you understand," she said. "But he'd come home with fresh marks on his face or hands, and he would be limping a lot too."

"Was he Irish?" James asked. With each thing she said, he was becoming more and more intrigued by this Olocher person.

"No, he's English."

"Did he have scars on his face?"

"Yes!" she answered, her eyes opening wider than before. "One on each cheek!"

"Did he get them while living with you?"

"No, he said someone robbed him and did it to him in England." That truth told by Olocher was the one that made up James' mind. Even after hearing about the scars on the man's face, he wasn't fully sure, but now he was.

In his investigation of the Cary Brothers's deaths, he learned about their past in England and it had been well known that the slicing of the cheeks of their victims was one of their ways of behaving. His hunch about the Cary Brothers's being a revenge killing fell neatly into place, as did his other theory that this enable him to kill again afterwards.

After some questions about each of the women who had been attacked, and finding Paulina knew nothing about them in relation to dates, James moved back to ask about the brothers' murders.

"Did you notice anything odd in Mr Olocher around the time of the murders of the Cary Brothers?" She shook her head in the same way she'd been doing to most of his questions so far, but then at the last moment and spark of recognition showed in her face.

"Wait!" she said, looking triumphant, "There was something odd about that time."

"What was it?" James asked eagerly.

"Thomas came home very late. I never heard him coming in, but the next morning he was odd and when I went in to change his water bowl, I couldn't find it at first."

"It was missing?"

"Yes, but I found it under his bed after a quick search."

"Under his bed?"

"Yes, and it was empty." James didn't know what this signified, and he waited for her to go on. "But there was a stain around the rim the likes of which I'd never seen at that time but have come to know well since."

"What was it?" he asked, knowing the answer but longing to hear it said.

"Blood," she said grimly, "and worse that time than any other I found blood in it."

"This happened a lot?"

"Not like that time; he never hid it again, but he was in so many fights there was always a little blood when he washed of his face or hands."

"I can see why you got rid of him," James said, tutting and then asked, "Do you know where he is now?"

"No, but I know he's still around. I see him from time to time as I go about my business in the mornings."

"Locally?"

"Yes, always close to here."

"Thank you," James said. "You have been most helpful. Now if you can just give me a more detailed description of Mr Olocher, I will be on my way."

James left triumphant, knowing he had this man. He'd worried that whoever it was had fled by now, especially after the killing of Lee outside James' own home. He'd assumed this was because the man had known what Lee was going to tell the Alderman. It seemed that he was still around and it now only a matter of time before James got a hold of him.

CHAPTER 22

The fever Thomas Olocher had feared came the day after he killed Lee. It was the ill-advised dip in the river to cleanse himself of the blood that had done it. He took to his bed and, for the next couple of days, knew very little of what was real and what was imagined. The people he'd killed and some he'd only fought with came to him and he couldn't tell if this was in a dream or in fact. Now and then, the drunken lamentations of Tymon would puncture the shapes and bodies that danced about the room.

"Eat this if you want to be better!" he yelled, and another time the gruff voice shouted, "Keep this on your head, you idiot!" and he felt a coldness slap against his forehead.

The Cary Brothers rose, and it was the first time they met now, and the two bandits had all the power. They sliced into his cheeks and for the first time he recalled this happening and felt the pain of it afresh. Paulina came to mind, looking down on him with pity; he tried to call out to her, but she couldn't hear him. He thought then that he was dead and wondered how it had happened.

Two days after falling into bed, his eyes opened, and he knew at once this was the real world once more. He looked around the room, seeing the door open and through it, Tymon sitting by the fire. The ever-present bottle in his hands. Olocher sat up and found that his body was stiff and sore and wondered how long he'd been out. Getting out of bed, he shuffled across the room, moving like he was a hundred years old. His legs felt like jelly, and he didn't know how long they were going to hold him up.

"You're alive then?" Tymon said, seeing him in the doorway.

"Looks like it," Olocher replied.

"I wasn't sure you'd make it," Tymon nodded and then went back to looking at the fire.

"How long was I sick?"

"Only a couple of days."

Thomas Olocher thought that this wasn't so bad when the memory of Philip Lee came back to him. He had to get out of the city; they were looking for a man with a scar on both cheeks. They were closing in.

"Anything in the pot?" he asked, knowing he would get nowhere before getting back into some kind of normal functioning.

"Stew," Tymon said, nodding.

Olocher ate greedily, seeing Tymon's disapproving glances at how much he was taking. Olocher ignored him. He would not have to put up with much more of the man's dour face, anyway. When he'd finished eating, he washed briefly and dressed up, wrapping up well both against the cold and to cover his face from the public. It was already late afternoon, and he was going to go to the docks and see if there was a ship leaving today he could be on.

Olocher only made it a couple of streets before he heard something that stopped him in his tracks. Two women spoke at a corner and though he knew neither of their names, he had seen them before and knew they lived in the building next to Paulina's.

"The Alderman was in with Paulina this morning," one said, "and he looked very happy when he was leaving."

"Why so?" the other asked.

"I think that strange creature that was living with her a while back is who the Alderman was looking for."

"And now he knows how he is?" the second woman asked excitedly.

"That's how it seemed to me," the first one said.

Olocher moved on, not wanting to look suspicious or draw their attention to himself. His heart sank at the idea that Paulina had done for him. How could she? His brief thoughts of how he once imagined them leaving together came back to mind, but it was fleeting. His anger was descending now, and there was no stopping the darkness rising.

His feet knew well enough the way that would take him back to his old lodgings, to his betrayer. Dusk was falling, and the streets were still busy with afternoon trade. His breath curled around him in hard clouds as he pushed on through the stiffness.

The ground floor door to the building was unlocked, as it always was during the day. As he walked up the stairs, his old feelings of being at home tried to invade his senses, but they were quickly turned again to anger and hatred. It was in this moment or utter fury that he looked up and his eyes — the only part of his face visible through the scarf — met those of Paulina. She had been on her way down, but when she saw him, she screamed and ran back up.

Olocher set after her, their speeds matched, but he knew she had nowhere to go. He heard the door to her rooms slam shut and the lock slide across. Olocher stopped on the top step and took in a deep breath. He looked around. No one had reacted to the scream. No door was ajar, that was visible to him.

He was about to knock on the door, to say something to Paulina, but the dark shape didn't allow it. It wanted blood, and it would not be denied any longer. Olocher's shoulder smashed heard in the door and it gave way at once. He almost fell into the room in surprise at how easy it had been.

Paulina stood before him, trembling and crying. A pang of sorrow rocked his heart, but his hands were not his own and they reached inside the pockets for the blades. Her eyes widened in horror as she saw them emerge and she had the look of one who knew their fate. She didn't scream as he came at her.

The attack was as vicious as any that had come before it and Paulina's body put up a fight, even if her mind already knew the outcome. She tried to crawl away as he sat exhausted and breathing hard on the floor beside her. She was cut so many times and there was so much blood that she couldn't move on it. She slipped and groaned in agony before feeling his weight on her back. His hands grasped her cheek and lifted her head, and she felt his hot breath in her ear.

"It didn't have to be like this," he whispered, and the surreal certainty that he was crying as he spoke came to her. The blade came across her throat and then all was gone.

Olocher left, his mind not yet his own, and no one challenged him on his way down. It would be hours before he was clear-headed enough to understand what he had done, and once he did, he cried heavily. His other clothes were gone, where he knew not, and the cold bit into him. He was going to make himself sick again if he didn't get home. There would be no ship to take him anywhere tonight, but he meant to be on one, going anywhere, the first thing in the morning.

CHAPTER 23

What Thomas Olocher didn't know, and something he would have thought about at the time had the darkness not consumed him, was that Paulina's murder had a witness. The young Mary Sommer's had seen it all from a kitchen cupboard. When Paulina rushed in, having seen Olocher on the stairs, her only thought was for the safety of the little girl. Taking hold of Mary, she pushed her into the cupboard and told her,

"No matter what you hear, don't come out of here or look out!" Mary nodded in terror; she had never seen her aunt like this before and she had no clue what was going on. "I mean it, Mary, you have to promise me," Paulina said. Mary could only nod again before the door was shut closed on her.

Unfortunately, there was a small gap in the doors when they were closed, and Mary could see quite well through it. Though she knew she shouldn't look, she found it impossible not to, especially when she heard the front door crash open so violently.

It was a scene Mary would never forget for as long as she lived. How she stayed quiet was something she'd never understand, but she knew it had saved her life. Had he known she was there only a few feet behind him, Thomas Olocher would have killed her too.

With a bravery well beyond her years, Mary left the closet only a few moments after the killer had left it. One look at her aunt told her the woman was dead, but she knew she had to raise the alarm. Running down to the street, she saw Olocher round the corner before she set off after him. She had to keep him in sight until she could tell a soldier or someone in authority what had happened.

This turned out to be a longer spell than Mary had imagined. Street after street passed and there was no sign of anyone she could tell. She saw Olocher pull off his coat and toss in into a fire barrel some men had at a corner. They looked at him with surprise, but he just kept on going. Further on, he took off his scarf, and that too was tossed into a passing cart. She saw him run his hands along wet window ledges and using the water to rub his hands together and wash off the blood.

Mary found that she couldn't take her eyes off him for long periods. It was possible at these times she had walked right past a soldier on duty or someone from the Parish Watch. Hours passed in this constant walk, with seemingly no route in mind. She saw that they passed the same places many times. As fate would have it, the person she ran into who could help her was Alderman James himself.

"Are you alright, little girl?" he asked on seeing her look of recognition of him. She was shivering and wasn't dressed to be out in such weather as this.

"Thomas Olocher," she pointed. "He killed my aunt!" at the utterance of these words, Mary broke down sobbing. James took hold of her and looked where she pointed. He saw the man and knew he had to get after him. Olocher wasn't running, however. Taking his cloak off, he wrapped Mary in it and said,

"Get yourself in somewhere warm, I'll get him."

James set off after the man he now was sure was the killer. As he closed the distance on Olocher, James noticed that he seemed completely oblivious to his surroundings and never once looked behind. Drawing nearer still, he saw the quickly rising and falling shoulders of his prey. At first, he didn't know what this was, but when he heard the guttural noises that went along with it, he understood. The man was sobbing almost uncontrollably. At least this was something, James thought. He felt something about what he did.

James followed for a time, not sure what to do. He didn't want to try to apprehend this crazed killer alone, but also, he did not want the man to be roaming free, either. Who knew when he might take a notion and attack someone who was passing by?

Soon, James saw that they would pass the gate of Newgate Prison. This was where he could get some help. Olocher passed by the gate and James rushed up and knocked on them. A man appeared at the slot and on seeing who it was, started to open up.

"Get two men out here to help me," James said, "and hurry, he's getting too far away!" Thankfully for James, the guard did not dither in asking questions and called out two names. "Tell them to follow me down this way," James pointed, "I will look out for them."

James rushed in to close the gap on Olocher once more. The two men soon joined him and they came up on Olocher just as he turned to enter a building.

"Stop there, Mr Olocher," James said. "It's all over."

The face that turned to look on James was almost one of relief, but it quickly turned to gruff anger.

"What are you talking about?" Olocher snapped. "Who are you?"

"I am Alderman James, and these men are from Newgate Prison. I am placing you under arrest for multiple murders and assaults in Dublin city over the last few months."

"Who's murder? I never hurt anyone in my life!"

"The Cary Brother's amongst others," James said, and he nodded for the two men to take hold of Olocher.

Thomas Olocher's hands had been his pockets for this entire conversation and just as the men put their hands out to take hold of his arms, his hands shot out with a knife in each and cut at the men's arms.

"Look out!" one of them shouted, and then both groaned in pain and backed away. James felt the thud of Olocher's boot into his stomach, but he'd seen it coming and he swung his own cane up at the same time and caught Olocher heavily under the jaw. The murderer's eyes rolled in his head and James followed up with a sideways crack across Olocher's face, that sent him sprawling to the ground. The men, despite their bleeding arms, jumped down and pinned both of Olocher's hand, shaking the blades clear.

"Like I said, Olocher," James said, fixing his coat. "It's all over."

CHAPTER 24

The trial of Thomas Olocher was one that everyone in the city took a keen interest in. Every night the coffee houses, taverns and Whiskey Cabins would be full of reports of what had gone on in court day. People would lay claim to the fact that they knew all along what Olocher really was, and others would deny ever knowing the man. Many more would tell tales of how they were lucky to be alive, having come under the fists and blades of Thomas Olocher. Some of these stories were made up or else exaggerated, but some were true.

It would pain Mary Sommer's if she knew what salacious gossip was passing for truth in some quarters. There were stories of an affair, of love between Paulina and Olocher. It had turned bad, so the story went, and she put him out. He didn't like this and made sure she paid for it. Other said she knew all along what he had been doing and only turned him in because she feared for her own life.

Though no one in the city felt in any doubt as to whether or not Olocher was a killer, they all laughed along as the news reports of his denials came in day by day. Witnesses talked of him sitting in court like a Lord, his nose turned up at the proceedings. He would admit to nothing and claimed he had nothing to with any crime whatsoever, let alone one so egregious as murder.

It was to be the testimony of the frail young Mary Sommers that would do Olocher in finally. Her words and tears were so powerful that no one who heard her could think to deny them. Hers were not the only tears in the courtroom that day.

Olocher's own wild fighting and attacking style also testified against him. The judge made him show his bare thighs were all the old cut marks from his own blades were on display. Despite that, he did not admit to anything.

Thomas Olocher was found guilty and sentenced to hang the next morning. The judge ordered that he be sent to Newgate Prison, or the 'Black Dog' as it was known locally. This seemed an odd choice, as it was generally a debtor's prison that also held prostitutes in the basement level. Few killers had seen the inside of it. The general opinion was that the prison was getting the dubious 'honour' of housing him on his last night as guards from there had been instrumental in Olocher's arrest.

Alderman James was happy with the result of the case. He knew Olocher was the man and was relieved that the judge agreed. He looked into the condemned man's eyes as he was led away and Olocher stopped and said to him,

"This isn't over, yet, Alderman." James didn't respond. He simply nodded to the men to take him away on his trip to Newgate. He would be dead by early morning of the next day, and James had nothing else to say to him.

That night, wet from the rain and getting colder as the hours passed by, Thomas Olocher sat in the high tower cell of Newgate Prison. His bed was low and barely covered with hay, none of which was fresh. The rain still fell outside, and the wind howled through the bars. The anger of his sentence had turned to sorrow for himself. His body was bruised from the treatment of the soldiers, and his mind could think about things for only a few moments before the gallows would come back to the forefront. How had things come to this?

For the first time in years, he thought about his father. He wasn't even sure if the old man was still alive, but Olocher saw him tutting and shaking his head if he knew where his son had ended up. Could even he have predicted how far Erskine Chambers would fall? Olocher smiled ruefully at the thought of his old name.

"You never did make all that money you said you would," he said to himself, shaking his head. Tears came to his eyes and fell. He was afraid now, more afraid than he had ever been in his life.

As he wept, he heard some odd noises from outside the wall of the prison. Going to the window, he looked down at the main gates out in the courtyard. He could see the gate begin to bulge under some force and beyond the gates, in the street, he could see loads of pigs. He had never seen so many pigs in all his life in one place. They were a common nuisance on the streets in Dublin, but he never thought there were this many. They seemed to be getting whipped up into some kind of frenzy too, and this was something else Olocher had never seen or heard of. What on earth was going on? It was getting louder and louder down there.

This is when he heard his name being called.

"Olocher!" Looking down into the alleyway on the other side of the prison walls, he saw someone down there. He pressed his head to the bars to try to see better. As he did, he saw that it was Cleaves; one of the few drinking buddies he had who he'd never had call to fight with.

"What is it?" he called down, the pigs still shrilling at the gate.

"Take this," Cleave said, and Olocher saw him toss something up. He pulled his head back just in time to see a heavy handled knife come in through the bars. He looked down at Claves once more. "Make good use of it." Cleaves said, and then he walked away.

Olocher picked up the knife, and it felt good in his hand. For an instant, the ideas of killing the guards who came for him in the morning and then anyone else who tried to stop him getting away flashed in his mind, but then he knew at once it was nonsense. He understood what Cleaves had meant by putting it to good use.

How would the darkness in him feel about this, about not getting all those guards in an attempted escape?

It turned out that the darkness didn't care; it was as easy to pull the blade across his own throat as it had been on anyone else's.

Read a Free Sample of 'The Dolocher' here

The End

A Clattering of Jackdaws

A Kettle of Hawks

A Clamour of Rooks

A Fall of Woodcocks

The Birdwatcher Boxset

The Legend of Long Jones

The Coroner

The Red Scowl